ANGELFISH MAKO SHARK GREAT WHITE SHARK MANTA RAY WHALE SHARK

COOKIE CUTTER SHARK MORAY EEL HAMMERHEAD SHARK FLASHLIGHT FISH JELLYFISH

MANATEE SEA TURTLE SEA HORSE WALRUS SEA CUCUMBER

GIANT SQUID SEA OTTER HUMPBACK KILLER WHALE SCALLOP

DIVE INTO AN UNDERWATER ADVENTURE WITH...

A WORKBOOK FOR CHILDREN
GRADES 3–4

Author: Keith J. Suranna
Illustration: Joe Veno
Design: creatives, nyc
Editors: Carol Pugliano, Leslie Goldman

A GOLDEN BOOK•NEW YORK
Golden Books Publishing Company, New York, New York 10106

Year: 1866

Dear _____,
(write your name here)

Hello and welcome! The United States Navy and I are calling upon you for a most important and dangerous mission. We need your help in locating a mysterious sea creature that has been terrorizing the seven seas. This dreaded sea creature is reported to be over 300 feet long and has the power to rip a ship apart with its long, sharp nose. Are you interested in either finding this monster or proving it is a fake? If so, please agree to accept this mission.

Our expedition begins in New York Harbor aboard the warship USS *Abraham Lincoln*. I, Captain Farragut, the Navy officer in charge of the ship, am determined to find the monster and stop it once and for all. I have also asked the famous harpooner, Ned Land, to come on board and harpoon the beast when it is found.

Okay, in order to find this monster we should go to the last place it was spotted. It was last seen attacking a ship in the middle of the Atlantic Ocean. The captain of another ship saw the whole thing happen and has given us the coordinates of his location. I'll need your help in plotting our course to that spot.

Well, monster tracker, we're on our way. Turn the page to begin your tracking journey by learning about coordinates so that you can help me use the world map to plot the course of the USS *Abraham Lincoln*. Good luck. Let's get out there and find that beast!

Captain Farragut

Where in the World Are We?

Pull out the world map on page 30. Look at the letters and numbers across the bottom, top, and up and down the sides. By using these letters and numbers you can give the coordinates of places on the map. Coordinates tell us where something is located on a map.

To find the coordinates of New York Harbor, where the USS *Abraham Lincoln* is now located, put your finger on New York City. Move your finger straight up or down until you hit a letter. Did you hit the letter "G"? Good job! Now put your finger back on New York City and move straight across to the left or right, until you get to a number. Did you hit the number "4"? Good work! So now you know that the coordinates of New York City are G,4 on our map of the world. The letter always goes first, and the number goes second.

Draw a picture of the **USS Abraham Lincoln** *on New York City to show where your ship is located. Now try to find the coordinates of these places!*

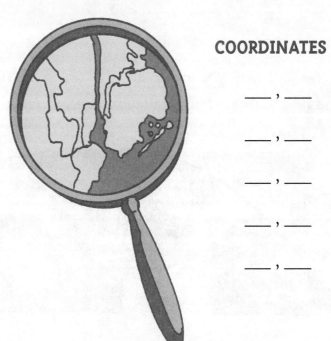

PLACE	COORDINATES
■ Cairo, Egypt	___ , ___
■ London, England	___ , ___
■ Quito, Ecuador	___ , ___
■ Paris, France	___ , ___
■ Tokyo, Japan	___ , ___

Finding Our Way

"Sometimes," says Captain Farragut, "a place does not line up exactly with a letter or number. When this happens, just use the number and letter that are closest to the place as the coordinates. And sometimes a place (like an ocean) is so big that it is more than one letter across and more than one number up and down. When this happens, pick the number and letter in the middle of the place."

Try these!

PLACE	COORDINATES
■ North Pacific Ocean	___ , ___
■ New Delhi, India	___ , ___
■ Baltic Sea	___ , ___
■ Reykjavík, Iceland	___ , ___
■ Canberra, Australia	___ , ___

Good job! Now you are ready to go on to the next page and help Captain Farragut locate the last place the monster was spotted!

Where To?

Location: New York Harbor   **Coordinates:** G,4

"Now," says Captain Farragut, "what if you know what the coordinates are, and you want to find the place? For example: If I go to the coordinates A,3, where will I be? To find out, put one finger on the A and one finger on the 3. Now, at the same time, slowly move your fingers up and across until they meet. Instead of starting at the place and finding the coordinate, you are starting at the coordinates and finding the place. Where did you end up? The Bering Sea? Great work, you are exactly right! Try these for practice!"

Hint: These are all bodies of water.

COORDINATES   **PLACE**

■ O,1   _____

■ U,10   _____

■ X,10   _____

■ G,3   _____

■ L,1   _____

We're on Our Way!

"Excellent work!" says Captain Farragut. "Now, look on your map and use your great map-reading skills to find out where the USS *Abraham Lincoln* should go to be at the place the sea monster was last spotted."

The *Abraham Lincoln* has arrived at the location where the monster was last seen. After days of seeing nothing but ocean, Ned Land yells, "There's the monster and it's coming right at us!" You brace yourself as the beast rams the ship.

You and Ned are knocked into the water. As you both swim for your lives, you climb up onto the monster. It is made of metal!

Where will the coordinates J,4 bring the USS *Abraham Lincoln?*

Mark an "X" in that place. Then draw a line from New York Harbor to the new location. Now you have started your map of our ship's course. Throughout your journey around the oceans and seas of the world, you will keep track of your path. Each time you reach a new location, mark an "X" in that spot and draw a line from your last location to the new one. At the bottom of almost every page in this book you will see a **Coordinate Clue***. This will give you a clue to figure out where your next destination will be. At the end of the book you will have a map covered in lines and "X's", showing all the places you have been on your adventure.*

Step by Step

Location: North Atlantic Ocean   **Coordinates:** J,4

"I think I see some kind of hatch on this thing," Ned says to you. As you open the hatch and look down, you see a metal ladder that leads down into darkness. Peering down you say, "Well, Ned what have we got to lose?" As Ned looks at you, he says, "You go first!"

To get down the ladder you must figure out the number pattern on the two ladders below. Using the numbers given to you, fill in the missing ones.

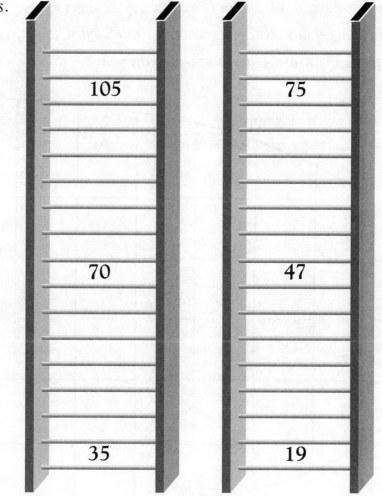

Coordinate Clue: The next location of the *Nautilus* is M,4. Where is this?

Finding Your Way

Location: Mediterranean Sea   **Coordinates:** M,4

At the bottom of the ladder there is a tall man with a black beard. "I am Captain Nemo. Welcome to my submarine, the *Nautilus*," the man says. "If you would like to stay, I have a private cabin for the both of you. You are free to explore the *Nautilus*, but I must warn you that it comes with a price." You and Ned decide to stay and Captain Nemo gives you a map of the submarine.

Follow the directions Captain Nemo gives you to get to your cabins. He may have you stop at other places so you'll learn your way around the Nautilus. Draw a line to mark your steps.

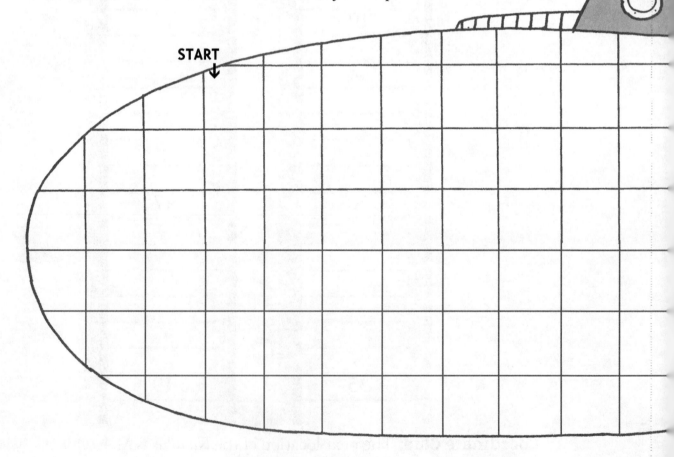

START
↓

1. Go south 2 squares.

2. Go east 3 squares and put an "X" here. This is the library.

3. Go south 2 squares.

4. Go east 4 squares.

5. Go north 2 squares and put an "X" here. This is the art gallery.

6. Go east 1 square.

7. Go south 2 squares.

8. Go west 2 squares and put an "X" here. This is the kitchen.

9. Go west 7 squares and put a "star" here. This is your cabin.

Enjoy your stay!

C.N.

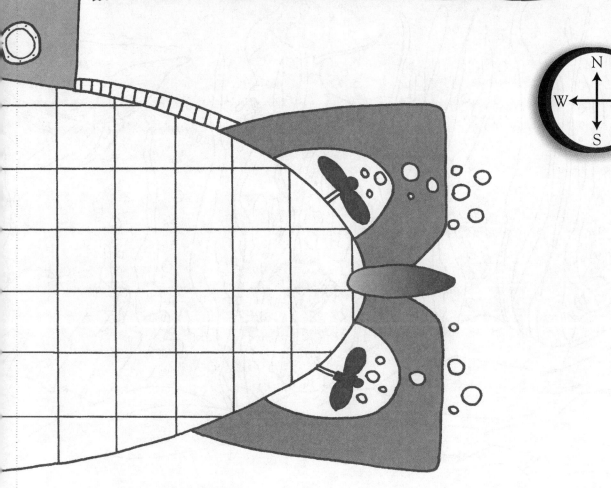

Coordinate Clue: The next destination for the *Nautilus* is O,4.

The Hidden World

Location: Black Sea

Coordinates: O,4

After being aboard the *Nautilus* for a few days, you are amazed at what you have seen. As you peer out of one of the portholes you observe underwater creatures of all kinds. "Simply amazing," you say to yourself.

Find the 10 hidden sea creatures. When you find an animal, put the sticker of that animal on top of its picture.

Animals to be found:

- octopus
- jellyfish
- sea horse
- moray eel
- manta ray

- sea cucumber
- swordfish
- sea otter
- porcupine fish
- true crab

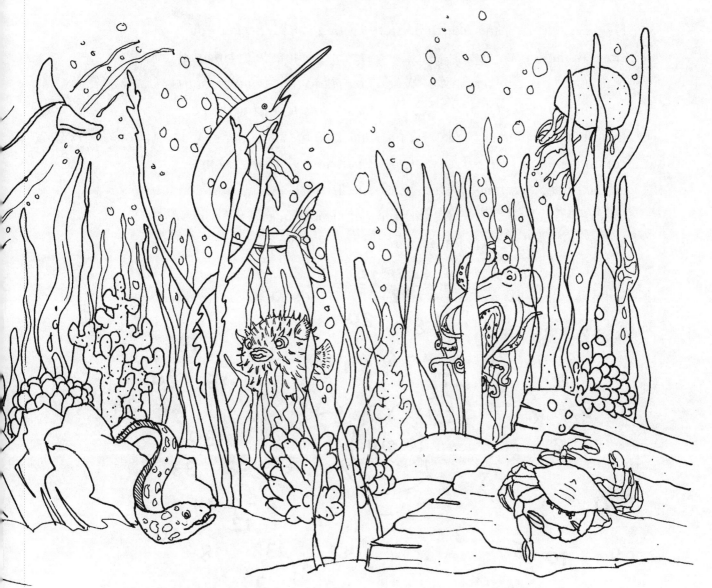

Coordinate Clue: The next location for the *Nautilus* is off the Canary Islands. What are those coordinates?

Uncovering Mysteries

Location: Canary Islands,
North Atlantic Ocean

Coordinates: K,5

After your outdoor adventure, you and Ned continue to explore
the wonders of the *Nautilus*. "What could this be?" Ned asks, as
he comes across a strange sight. "Help me figure this out."

*Help Ned discover this hidden mystery. With a pencil, begin at the
circle. Counting by twos (2,4,6,8,etc.), draw a line following the
path that these numbers make. When you get to the diamond, start
counting by threes (3,6,9,12,etc.). Draw a line following the path
that the these numbers make. At the square do the same thing,
counting by fours (4,8,12,16,etc.). When you get to the triangle,
do the same, counting by fives (5,10,15,20,etc.). At the star, count
by sixes (6,12,18,24,etc.) until your path leads back to the circle.
What mystery have you uncovered?*

Coordinate Clue: The next location of the *Nautilus* is F,5.

Tentacles!

Location: Gulf of Mexico   **Coordinates:** F,5

You and Ned discover that Captain Nemo has an octopus tank aboard the *Nautilus*. "What a huge tank," you say. "It must fit 12 octopuses!" "I wonder how many tentacles that is," Ned says. So, you and Ned decide to figure that out.

Use multiplication to find out how many tentacles there are for each group of octopuses. The first two are done for you.

OCTOPUSES IN THE TANK	TENTACLES ON EACH
1	1 X 8 = 8
2	2 X 8 = 16
3	
4	
5	
6	
7	
8	
9	
10	
11	
12	

Coordinate Clue: Your next destination is G,6. Where are you now?

How Long Has It Been?

Location: Caribbean Sea   **Coordinates:** G,6

You discover that Captain Nemo's price for exploring the *Nautilus* is that you and Ned have to spend the rest of your lives aboard the submarine! "I'm getting sick of being inside this sardine can," Ned says to you. "We've been aboard the *Nautilus* for so long that I've lost track of time!"

Help Ned make up for lost time by circling the correct clock below.

■ You boarded the USS *Abraham Lincoln* at 8:00 P.M.

■ The monster struck the *Abraham Lincoln* at 10:15 A.M.

■ At half-past one in the afternoon, you and Ned discovered that the monster was really the *Nautilus*.

■ You took a nap in your cabin at three quarters past one in the afternoon.

Coordinate Clue: The *Nautilus* is heading for K,9.

Nemo's Secret Language

Location: South Atlantic Ocean   **Coordinates:** K,9

> One thing that you've noticed while you have been aboard the *Nautilus* is that Captain Nemo speaks to his crew in a language you've never heard before. Because you are naturally curious, you decide to decode it.

By comparing the unknown symbols of Nemo's language to the alphabet, decode what he is saying.

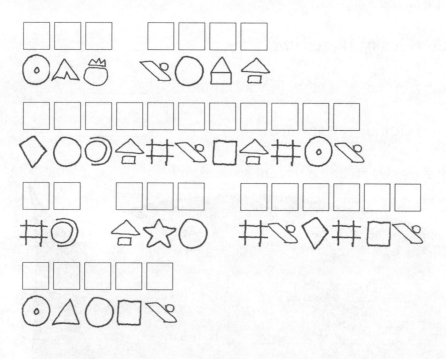

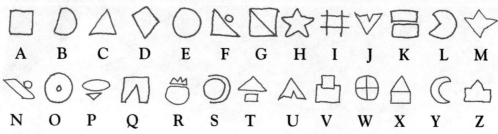

Coordinate Clue: R,7. Where are we going?

Measuring Captain Nemo's Way

Location: Indian Ocean   **Coordinates:** R,7

On the *Nautilus*, you discover that Captain Nemo and his crew have their own way of measuring things. Their unit of measurement is fish!

Below is the fish they use to measure. Trace it on a separate piece of paper and cut it out. Use this fish to measure the following things by Captain Nemo's system. (If it is not exactly a fish long, you can estimate to the nearest half-fish.)

■ How many fish long is your arm?   _____

■ How many fish long is a table in your home?   _____

■ How many fish long is your shoe?   _____

* *Now pick three other items you want to measure!*

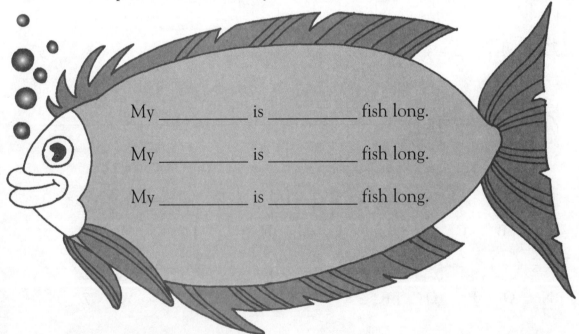

My _____ is _____ fish long.

My _____ is _____ fish long.

My _____ is _____ fish long.

Coordinate Clue: The next destination for the Nautilus is X,5. Locate this place on your map.

Dividing Dinner

Location: South Pacific Ocean   **Coordinates:** X,5

> "Good fishing!" Captain Nemo exclaims. "There's only one problem. Our chef is a great cook, but sometimes he has trouble with division. He needs your help to figure out these problems. Otherwise we might not get dinner at all!"

1. The nets have brought in 120 jellyfish. The chef wants to make juicy jellyfish jigglers, for 30 people. How many jellyfish should he put in each person's jiggler?

_____

2. Luscious lumpfish is very rare. For every 20 fish the *Nautilus* nets catch, only 1 is a lumpfish. If the nets caught 200 fish today, how many lumpfish will the chef have to cook?

_____

3. After everyone eats their stingray lips and octopus eyes, there are 40 dirty dishes. If the *Nautilus* has 5 crew members who are dishwashers, how many dishes will each of them have to wash?

_____

4. One of the dishwashers gets indigestion from bad eel sausage and now there are only 4 dishwashers. If there are 32 dirty dishes left, how many will each of them have to wash?

_____

5. For dessert, the chef has prepared 5 sea cucumber cakes. Into how many pieces will each cake need to be cut? Remember, there are 30 people on board.

_____

Coordinate Clue: Nemo informs you that the *Nautilus* is heading toward the Galapagos Islands in the Pacific Ocean.

Sea Creatures Galore

Location: Galapagos Islands, Pacific Ocean   **Coordinates:** E,8

> "Professor," Ned says, "we've seen some wonderful sea animals, but I don't know a thing about them. How can I learn more?"

Help Ned learn more about sea animals. Match each sea animal with its characteristics. Put the sticker of the sea animal on top of its name.

1. STARFISH

a. pouches under eyes light up to frighten predators

2. SEA TURTLE

b. has five or more arms, crawls along bottom of the sea

3. GIANT SQUID

c. an arctic mammal, male has one long twisted tusk

4. NARWHAL

d. lays eggs on land, has a toothless beak and hard shell

5. FLASHLIGHT FISH

e. can weigh up to 3,000 pounds, has long front tusks

6. WALRUS

f. has very long body and ten arms, has rounded fins

Coordinate Clue: Your next location is A,3.

Nemo's Log

Location: Bering Sea   **Coordinates:** A,3

As you and Ned are exploring the bridge of the *Nautilus*, Ned yells, "Check this out!" You see that Ned is pointing to Nemo's captain's log where he has written everything about the *Nautilus*. "Let's read it to see what Nemo has in store for us," says Ned. Knowing you shouldn't be reading it, your curiosity gets the better of you as you open the log.

You discover that Nemo's log has a lot of mistakes. Correct the log. Look for spelling and punctuation mistakes. There are 22 mistakes in all.

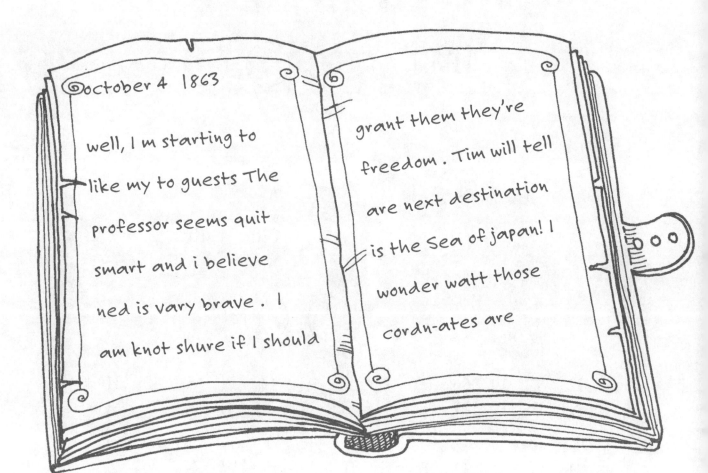

october 4 1863

well, I m starting to like my to guests The professor seems quit smart and i believe ned is vary brave . I am knot shure if I should grant them they're freedom . Tim will tell are next destination is the Sea of japan! I wonder watt those cordn-ates are

Coordinate Clue: The Nautilus is headed for V,4. Where is this?

Unlocking Nemo's Safe

Location: Sea of Japan   **Coordinates:** V,4

You and Ned have made another discovery! You have found Captain Nemo's secret safe. His combination is double coded by multiplication and the alphabet. To open the safe you need to solve the multiplication problems and then match the numbers in the answer to letters of the alphabet. When you break both codes you will find out what's in the safe. The first one is done for you as an example.

6	10	9	5	8	6
x 4	x 6	x 8	x 4	x 5	x 3
24					

(P) ( ) ( ) ( ) ( ) ( )

4	9	20	8
x 3	x 5	x 2	x 7

( ) ( ) ( ) ( )

12	15	11	20	10	9
x 9	x 4	x 5	x 3	x 4	x 2

( ) ( ) ( ) ( ) ( ) ( )

72	82	19	56	60	2	12	93	14	108	5	40	21
A	B	C	D	E	F	G	H	I	J	K	L	M

3	45	24	9	20	18	7	30	1	55	100	69	75
N	O	P	Q	R	S	T	U	V	W	X	Y	Z

Coordinate Clue: Find the place with the coordinates U,6.

Dolphins and Us

Location: South China Sea   **Coordinates:** U,6

You've become curious about the differences and similarities between people and sea animals.

Read the sentences below. Then fill in the Venn Diagram to explain the differences and similarities between you and a dolphin. A few are done for you.

- Dolphins live in the ocean.
- Humans live on land.
- Both humans and dolphins are mammals.
- Both humans and dolphins have lungs and nostrils to help them breathe air.
- Dolphins and humans are warm-blooded.
- Dolphins use their fins to help them swim.
- Humans use their arms and legs to help them move around.

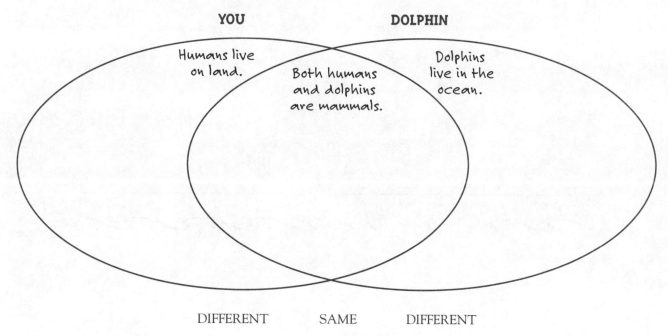

YOU   DOLPHIN

Humans live on land.

Both humans and dolphins are mammals.

Dolphins live in the ocean.

DIFFERENT   SAME   DIFFERENT

Coordinate Clue: Have you ever heard of the place with X,8 as its coordinates?

Sea Creature Features

Location: Coral Sea   **Coordinates:** X,8

> You discover that sea creatures have many things in common.
> But they can also be very different from one another.

*Choose from the animal list and put the sticker of each creature
where it belongs.*

ANIMALS WITH FINS

Animal list:

- sea urchin
- scallop
- marlin
- barracuda
- hermit crab

- sea snail
- whale shark
- tuna
- sea lily
- angelfish

- mako shark
- bluefish
- mole crab
- anemone
- hammerhead shark

ANIMALS WITH SHELLS	ANIMALS THAT LOOK LIKE PLANTS

Coordinate Clue: Nemo yells, "Take us to S,6!"

The Long and the Short of the Sea

Location: Bay of Bengal   **Coordinates:** S,6

> Throughout your trip you've been taking notes on different lengths and how they compare to each other. You decide to graph your research for future study.

Create a bar graph using the information below, then answer the questions. Captain Nemo is done for you.

Captain Nemo 6 feet; **Whale Shark** 40 feet; **Moray Eel** 6 feet; **Bull Shark** 10 feet; **Manatee** 13 feet; **Harbor Seal** 5 feet; **Seahorse** 5 inches.

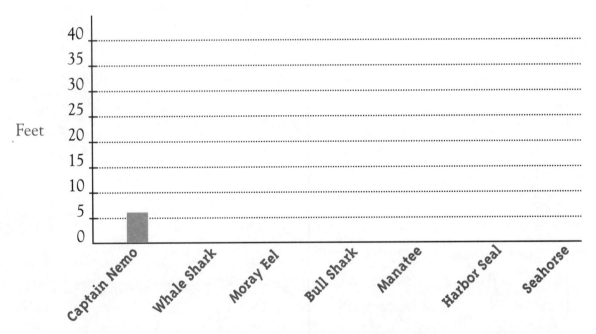

- Which is the longest?_____
- Which is the shortest?_____
- Which is the same height as Nemo? _____
- Which is the closest in length to the manatee?_____

Coordinate Clue: What are the coordinates for Madagascar?

Ned's Exam

Location: Madagascar   **Coordinates:** P,8

> "Well, Ned," Captain Nemo says, "in order to earn your freedom, it's time to find out what you've learned while being aboard the *Nautilus*!" "Hey," Ned replies, "I didn't know I was going to be tested on all this!"

Fill in the missing words in each sentence. Choose from the word list. Hint: Not all the words will be used.

Word list: maps, dolphin, harpoon, seahorse, 1967, sword, kelp, coordinates, whale, seaweed, anemone, 1997, funny, 1866, mysterious, manatee

1. If you were trying to get somewhere by looking at a map, the _____ would help you know where you're going.

2. The _____ is only 5 inches long.

3. Captain Nemo is a very _____ man. Most people know very little about him.

4. Your journey takes place a long time ago. In the year _____ you started out aboard the USS *Abraham Lincoln*.

5. The _____ lives in water, but breathes air through nostrils just like people.

Coordinate Clue: Find the coordinates for Buenos Aires, Argentina.

Shark Alley

Location: Buenos Aires, Argentina   **Coordinates:** I,9

"Well, you passed my little test," Nemo says to you and Ned. "But, if you want your freedom that badly, you must pass safely through Shark Alley! If you survive, I'll set you free, but if you don't, well . . ."

To safely get through Shark Alley you'll need 1 coin. On each move, flip the coin. If your coin lands on heads, move forward 2 spaces, but if your coin lands on tails, move backward 1 space. You must also read all the shark facts as you move along each space. Good luck!

Cookie Cutter: They are only 2 feet long. They love to eat blubber and will attack whales and other large sea animals. They take bites in neat round holes, like a cookie cutter.

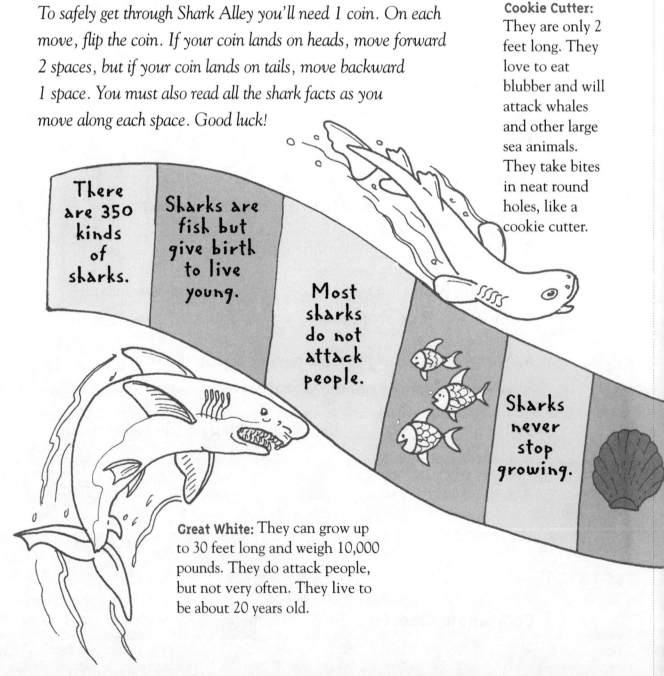

There are 350 kinds of sharks.

Sharks are fish but give birth to live young.

Most sharks do not attack people.

Sharks never stop growing.

Great White: They can grow up to 30 feet long and weigh 10,000 pounds. They do attack people, but not very often. They live to be about 20 years old.

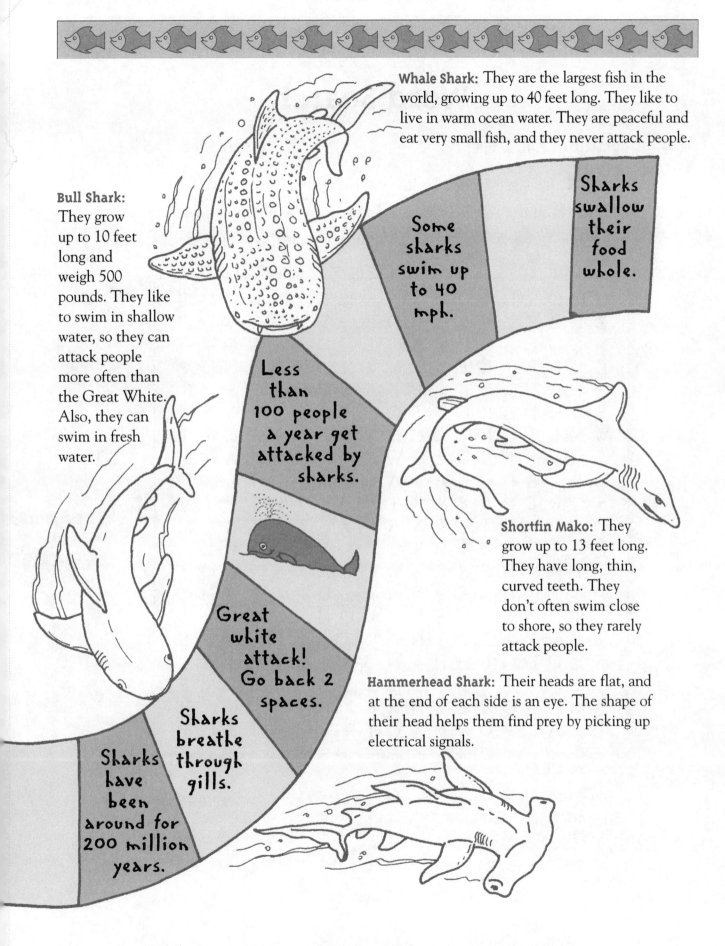

Whale Shark: They are the largest fish in the world, growing up to 40 feet long. They like to live in warm ocean water. They are peaceful and eat very small fish, and they never attack people.

Bull Shark: They grow up to 10 feet long and weigh 500 pounds. They like to swim in shallow water, so they can attack people more often than the Great White. Also, they can swim in fresh water.

Some sharks swim up to 40 mph.

Sharks swallow their food whole.

Less than 100 people a year get attacked by sharks.

Great white attack! Go back 2 spaces.

Sharks breathe through gills.

Sharks have been around for 200 million years.

Shortfin Mako: They grow up to 13 feet long. They have long, thin, curved teeth. They don't often swim close to shore, so they rarely attack people.

Hammerhead Shark: Their heads are flat, and at the end of each side is an eye. The shape of their head helps them find prey by picking up electrical signals.

Coordinate Clue: The *Nautilus* is now speeding toward O,5.

Word Search

Location: Cairo, Egypt　　　　　　　　**Coordinates:** O,5

You've experienced a lot of great things during your journey. Find the words below so that you can remember all you've seen. The words go up, down, backward, forward, and diagonally.

```
C O O R D I N A T E S R E T S N O M G
Z S Z E Y V F L P O E Q X T M Y B D C
N E D L A N D R A G I N D I A N O I A
D D H P I K F V C L J X O N L C U U P
E G N M A D K P F E A S M M S E S Q T
E R U L A R C T I C D M B J E X W S A
W N E W Q N R O C N J S L N A N H T I
A M L F L K T Z C W T W A C U J A N N
E P T A D Q K A R A I E C O R I L A N
S Q R E D S E A R T N E K Y C T E I E
O O U H B I L F X A L Y S W H T R G M
C U T V Z O I H R C Y K E D I F D L O
T E A M S S X R B O C E A N N V A G S
O W E X H N E F Y A M J U B C E Y H O
P J S Z W T K E L P L C H A S R D B Y
U P L E I F D I N A U T I L U S T S S
S V G D O L P H I N G W I R H O I A T
J I E U J E L L Y F I S H C K L F M E
N M O B Q V E S H A R K H P Z Q Q S R
T H A R P O O N N C I T N A L T A G V
```

NAUTILUS	NED LAND	WHALE	DOLPHIN
SEA TURTLE	MANTA RAY	SEA URCHIN	CORAL
STARFISH	SHARK	GIANT SQUID	MONSTER
SEAL	OCTOPUS	ANEMONE	OCEAN
HARPOON	JELLYFISH	ATLANTIC	BLACK SEA
INDIAN	ARCTIC	MEDITERRANEAN	BALTIC
RED SEA	KELP	SEAWEED	COORDINATES

There is also a secret bonus. Can you find it?

Remembering Your Journey

As you approach the end of your adventure, you say good-bye to Captain Nemo. You think back to the beginning of your journey in New York Harbor and how you are now ending up in Cairo, Egypt. In your notebook, you decide to write a poem about your wonderful sea journey.

Write one or more poems below about your journey. Remember, not all poems rhyme. Some words you might include in your poem are: Nemo, Ned Land, Nautilus, submarine, sea otter, kelp, harpoon, ocean, Tasman Sea, map, jellyfish, coordinates, walrus.

_____

_____

_____

_____

_____

_____

_____

_____

Map with coordinates

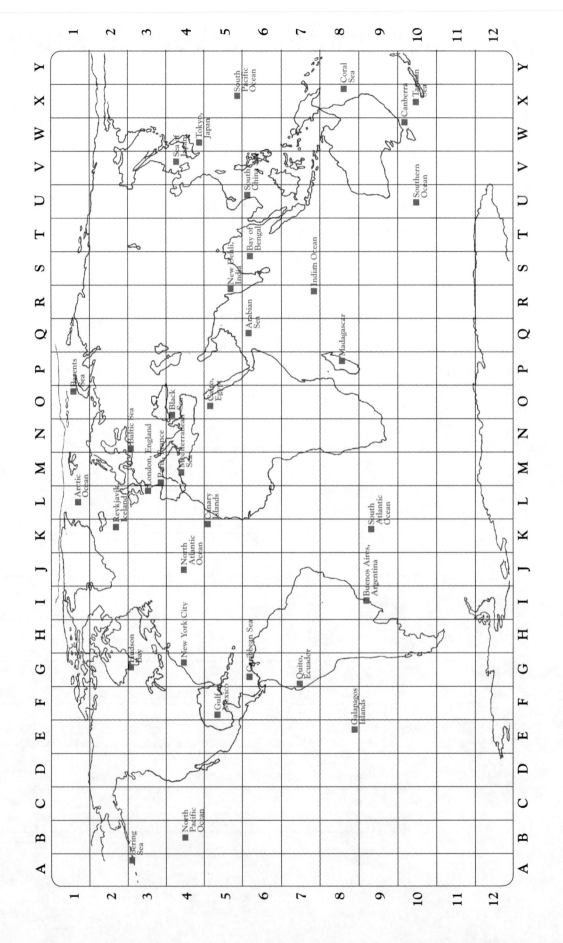

Answer Key

Where in the World Are We? — page 3

Cairo, Egypt	O,5
London, England	L,3
Quito, Ecuador	G,7
Paris, France	M,3
Tokyo, Japan	W,4

Finding Our Way — page 4

North Pacific Ocean	B,4
New Delhi, India	R,5
Baltic Sea	N,3
Reykjavík, Iceland	K,2
Canberra, Australia	W,10

Where To? — page 5

O,1	Barents Sea
U,10	Southern Ocean
X,10	Tasman Sea
G,3	Hudson Bay
L,1	Arctic Ocean

Step by Step — page 7

1st ladder:
Counting by fives

2nd ladder:
Counting by fours

105	75
100	71
95	67
90	63
85	59
80	55
75	51
70	47
65	43
60	39
55	35
50	31
45	27
40	23
35	19

The Hidden World — page 10, 11

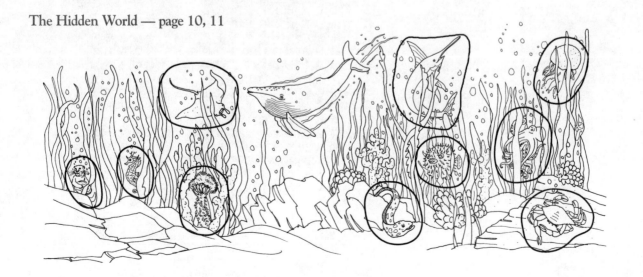

Uncovering Mysteries — page 12

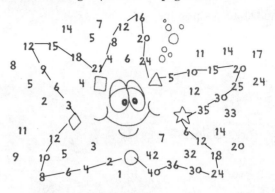

Tentacles! — page 13

1	1x8=8
2	2x8=16
3	3x8=24
4	4x8=32
5	5x8=40
6	6x8=48
7	7x8=56
8	8x8=64
9	9x8=72
10	10x8=80
11	11x8=88
12	12x8=96

How Long Has It Been? — page 14

Nemo's Secret Language — page 15

OUR NEXT DESTINATION IS THE
INDIAN OCEAN

Dividing Dinner — page 17

1. 4
2. 10
3. 8
4. 8
5. 6

Sea Creatures Galore— page 18

1. b
2. d
3. f
4. c
5. a
6. e

Nemo's Log— page 19

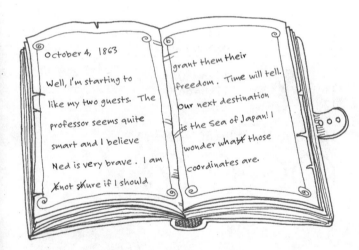

October 4, 1863

Well, I'm starting to like my two guests. The professor seems quite smart and I believe Ned is very brave. I am not sure if I should grant them their freedom. Time will tell. Our next destination is the Sea of Japan! I wonder what those coordinates are.

Unlocking Nemo's Safe — page 20

24	60	72	20	40	18
P	E	A	R	L	S

12	45	40	56
G	O	L	D

108	60	55	60	40	18
J	E	W	E	L	S

Dolphins and Us — page 21

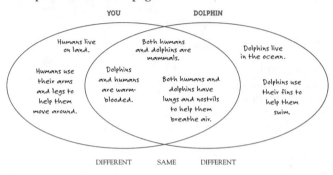

The Long and the Short of the Sea — page 24

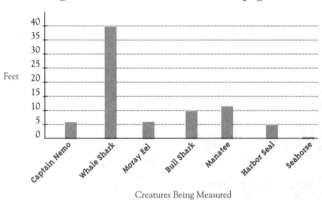

Creatures Being Measured

Ned's Exam — page 25

1. coordinates
2. seahorse
3. mysterious
4. 1866
5. dolphin

Word Search — page 28

MARLIN   SWORDFISH   TUNA   TRUE CRAB   NARWHAL

SEA LILY   SEA URCHIN   BARRACUDA   ANEMONE   BLUEFISH

SPERM WHALE   ZEBRA FISH   ELECTRIC RAY   GUITAR FISH   HERMIT CRAB

STARFISH   SEA SNAIL   MOLE CRAB   OCTOPUS   PORCUPINE FISH